Dear Parents:

Congratulations! Your child is taking the first steps on an exciting journey. The destination? Independent reading!

STEP INTO READING® will help your child get there. The program offers five steps to reading success. Each step includes fun stories and colorful art or photographs. In addition to original fiction and books with favorite characters, there are Step into Reading Non-Fiction Readers, Phonics Readers and Boxed Sets, Sticker Readers, and Comic Readers—a complete literacy program with something to interest every child.

Learning to Read, Step by Step!

Ready to Read   Preschool–Kindergarten
• big type and easy words • rhyme and rhythm • picture clues
For children who know the alphabet and are eager to begin reading.

Reading with Help   Preschool–Grade 1
• basic vocabulary • short sentences • simple stories
For children who recognize familiar words and sound out new words with help.

Reading on Your Own   Grades 1–3
• engaging characters • easy-to-follow plots • popular topics
For children who are ready to read on their own.

Reading Paragraphs   Grades 2–3
• challenging vocabulary • short paragraphs • exciting stories
For newly independent readers who read simple sentences with confidence.

Ready for Chapters   Grades 2–4
• chapters • longer paragraphs • full-color art
For children who want to take the plunge into chapter books but still like colorful pictures.

STEP INTO READING® is designed to give every child a successful reading experience. The grade levels are only guides; children will progress through the steps at their own speed, developing confidence in their reading.

Remember, a lifetime love of reading starts with a single step!

BARBIE and associated trademarks and trade dress are owned by, and used under license from, Mattel.
©2021 Mattel.
www.barbie.com

Published in the United States by Random House Children's Books, a division of Penguin Random House LLC, 1745 Broadway, New York, NY 10019, and in Canada by Penguin Random House Canada Limited, Toronto.

Step into Reading, Random House, and the Random House colophon are registered trademarks of Penguin Random House LLC.

Visit us on the Web!
StepIntoReading.com
rhcbooks.com

Educators and librarians, for a variety of teaching tools, visit us at RHTeachersLibrarians.com

ISBN 978-0-593-30451-8 (trade) — ISBN 978-0-593-30452-5 (lib. bdg.)
Printed in the United States of America

10 9 8 7 6 5 4 3 2 1

Barbie™

YOU CAN BE A DOCTOR

By Elle Stephens
Illustrated by Dynamo Limited

Random House 🏠 New York

Barbie wants to be
a doctor.
She visits a local
doctor's office.

She meets a nurse
named Mira.
Barbie is going
to help.

A little girl named Lily is waiting with her father.

Lily is nervous.

Her arm is in a cast.

Barbie tells her

not to worry.

Lily smiles.

Nurse Mira comes
to get Barbie.

"See you soon!"

Barbie tells Lily.

Barbie follows
Nurse Mira.
She is ready
to help!

Barbie washes her hands.
Then she puts on a
lab coat.

Barbie helps Nurse Mira
with an exam.
She says hello
to a boy named Oliver.

Nurse Mira checks
Oliver's weight.
Barbie writes it down
on his chart.

Then they check
Oliver's height.
"You are getting tall!"
says Nurse Mira.

Next, Nurse Mira checks Oliver's blood pressure. She puts a cuff on Oliver's arm. She listens.

It is good.

Barbie writes it

on his chart.

Just then,

Dr. Vargas comes in.

She is ready

to see Oliver.

Dr. Vargas starts Oliver's exam. She uses a special tool to check his ears.

Then the doctor
asks Oliver questions.
They talk about exercise
and eating healthy.

Barbie listens
with Oliver's mom.
She is learning
so much!

Barbie follows Dr. Vargas
to another exam.

They check the chart
on the door.
Lily is the next patient!

Lily is ready
to get her cast off.

First, Dr. Vargas wants
to make sure Lily's
arm is healed.

Barbie takes Lily
to the X-ray room.
The X-ray will take
a picture of Lily's bone.

An X-ray tech
takes the X-rays.
"Great job!"
Barbie tells Lily.

Dr. Vargas looks
at the X-rays.
Lily's bone is
all better!

"Good news," says Barbie.
"We can take
your cast off!"

Dr. Vargas cuts the cast
with a special saw.
Then she uses a tool
to open it up.

Barbie helps take
off the cast.
Lily bends her arm
and wiggles her fingers.

Lily wants to keep her cast.

She asks Barbie to sign it.

Barbie helps Lily
pick a special prize.
Lily chooses a
purple bouncy ball.

Barbie loves helping
Dr. Vargas.
"You can be a
doctor, too!"
says Dr. Vargas.